NEW!
PAPIER-
MÂCHÉ

JUST ADD
WATER!

SCIENCE FAIR DAY

BY
Lynn Plourde

ILLUSTRATED BY
Thor Wickstrom

Dutton Children's Books

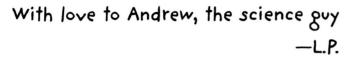

With love to Andrew, the science guy
—L.P.

To Sam, love always, Dad
—T.W.

DUTTON CHILDREN'S BOOKS A division of Penguin Young Readers Group
Published by the Penguin Group • Penguin Group (USA) Inc., 375 Hudson Street, New York, New York
10014, U.S.A. • Penguin Group (Canada), 90 Eglinton Avenue East, Suite 700, Toronto, Ontario, Canada
M4P 2Y3 (a division of Pearson Penguin Canada Inc.) • Penguin Books Ltd, 80 Strand, London WC2R
ORL, England • Penguin Ireland, 25 St Stephen's Green, Dublin 2, Ireland (a division of Penguin Books
Ltd) • Penguin Group (Australia), 250 Camberwell Road, Camberwell, Victoria 3124, Australia (a divi-
sion of Pearson Australia Group Pty Ltd) • Penguin Books India Pvt Ltd, 11 Community Centre, Panchsheel
Park, New Delhi – 110 017, India • Penguin Group (NZ), 67 Apollo Drive, Mairangi Bay, Auckland 1311, New
Zealand (a division of Pearson New Zealand Ltd) • Penguin Books (South Africa) (Pty) Ltd, 24 Sturdee
Avenue, Rosebank, Johannesburg 2196, South Africa • Penguin Books Ltd, Registered Offices: 80 Strand,
London WC2R ORL, England

Text copyright © 2008 by Lynn Plourde
Illustrations copyright © 2008 by Thor Wickstrom

Library of Congress Cataloging-in-Publication Data

Plourde, Lynn.
Science Fair Day / by Lynn Plourde; illustrated by Thor Wickstrom.—1st ed.
p. cm.
Summary: On Science Fair Day, Ima Kindanozee proves that she is the most inquisitive student
in Mrs. Shepherd's class.

ISBN 978-0-525-47878-2
[1. Science projects—Fiction. 2. Curiosity—Fiction. 3. Schools—Fiction.] I. Wickstrom, Thor, ill. II. Title.
PZ7.P724Sc 2008
[E]—dc22   2007018124

Published in the United States by Dutton Children's Books, a division of Penguin Young Readers Group
345 Hudson Street, New York, New York 10014
www.penguin.com/youngreaders

Designed by Irene Vandervoort

Manufactured in China   First Edition

3 5 7 9 10 8 6 4 2

It was Science Fair Day.
Everyone in Mrs. Shepherd's class was loaded down with
    posters and potions,
    gizmos and gadgets,
    chemicals and contraptions.
All the students were eager, excited, and anxious, especially . . .

Ima Kindanozee.

Ima liked to know anything and everything going on around her. She always asked plenty of questions. And the perfect day to ask questions was Science Fair Day.

"Did you make it?

"How's it work?

"What's this switch do?"
Ima asked Josephina.

"My, my," said Mrs. Shepherd. "How inventive, Josephina. This should be quite the Science Fair!"

Everyone joined the morning meeting circle. Well, almost everyone. Mrs. Shepherd looked around and asked, "Where's Ima?"

From a corner of the classroom, she heard some questions—which answered her own question.

"Why's it so big?
How's it stay together?
What's this bone connected to?"

CREAK-GROAN-CRASH!

"My, my," said Mrs. Shepherd. "How ambitious, Dewey. This really should be quite the—"

SQUEAK-SQUAWK-TALK. Just then the intercom interrupted her:

"Attention, please, this is Principal Helm speaking. As you all know, today is Science Fair Day. I shall be coming around to your classrooms to judge your projects. Please make certain they're all perfectly perfect."

Mrs. Shepherd nodded and said, "It does seem that some of your projects could use a few finishing touches."

Everyone got to work on their projects. Everyone, that is, except Ima Kindanozee.

She was too busy investigating Drew's project.

"Is that what one really looks like?

"What's it made of?

"Can it think?"

Drew said, "I forgot about making it until this morning. It isn't dry yet, so don't get too close—"
But it was already too late.

STICKY-ICKY-GOO!

"My, my," said Mrs. Shepherd. "How memorable, Drew.
This definitely should be quite the—"

RAP-TAP-SMACK. Someone was at the door.

"Yoo-hoo! Time to sneak a peek at all your perfectly perfect projects."

"Good morning, Principal Helm." said Mrs. Shepherd. "Our class isn't *quite* ready yet."

"Hmmm," said the principal. "That could be a problem. It will throw my schedule off by thirteen and a half minutes, but I guess I'll just have to come back later."

"Good idea," said Mrs. Shepherd. "When you return, there'll be much more to see."

Everyone got back to work on their projects. Even Ima headed toward hers, until she spied the most interesting project she'd seen so far.

IMA'S PROJECT DO NOT PEEK!

"Is it about food?
Or is it about colors?

"Or maybe it's about nature?" Ima interrogated Maybella.
"Yes! Yes! Yes!" answered Maybella. "I couldn't decide
which to do, so I did every one."
"And they all work together?" asked Ima.

FOOD IN NATURE

COLORS IN FOOD

NATURE IN COL

NOT
READY
DO NOT
TOUCH!!

"My, my," said Mrs. Shepherd. "Such a medley, Maybella. This definitely should be—"

RAP-TAP-SMACK. Someone was at the door again.

"Yoo-hoo. I'm baaaaaaaack!" said Principal Helm. "Ready or not, here I—"

When Principal Helm left, Mrs. Shepherd shook her head. "My, my, class, time's running out. Everyone, you really must get your projects ready.

"Let's check on yours," said Mrs. Shepherd as she led Ima over to her desk.

But when Ima pulled the cloth off, Mrs. Shepherd looked confused. "I don't understand. All you have are papers for your project?"

"Yup," said Ima. "I just couldn't stop thinking of questions and taking notes. I wrote everything down—all 999 pages of them."

"My, my," said Mrs. Shepherd. "That's so inquisitive, Ima. This definitely will be—"

RAP-TAP-SMACK . . .

"I WON'T GO. I WON'T TAKE NO FOR AN ANSWER—NOT THIS TIME!" exclaimed Principal Helm.

"Er . . . um . . . Come right in," Mrs. Shepherd said. "We've been waiting for you. You'll see we have quite the Science Fair to show you. Why don't you start over in this corner? Ima will give you the tour."

Ima and the principal began looking at all the projects. Ima not only took notes, but she asked some perfectly perfect questions.

"What makes the lava flow?"

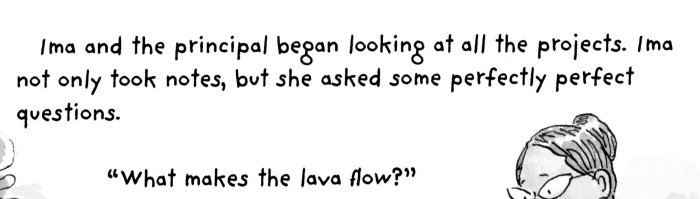

"How did that plant grow?"

"Why does that sun glow?"

"How does the hamster know?"

"My, my, Mrs. Shepherd, you're right. This really IS quite the perfectly perfect Science Fair," said Principal Helm as she handed out ribbon after ribbon after ribbon.

At last, everyone packed up their
posters and potions,
gizmos and gadgets,
chemicals and contraptions,
and headed home.

But as Ima began to pick up her papers, Mrs. Shepherd said, "I'm sorry you didn't get a ribbon, Ima, but you DO have something that no one else does."

"What's that?" asked Ima.